Finn-tastic Adventures

Jill Wilson

Illustrations by Dani Suhy

CROOKED TREE
STORIES

Published by Crooked Tree Stories of Ada, Michigan.
Direct inquiries to Betty Epperly at crookedtreestories.com

Dedicated to our grandson Finn —

His adventures began on June 1st, 2016, magical 6-1-16.

.

A bundle of joy with an amazing sense of wonder...

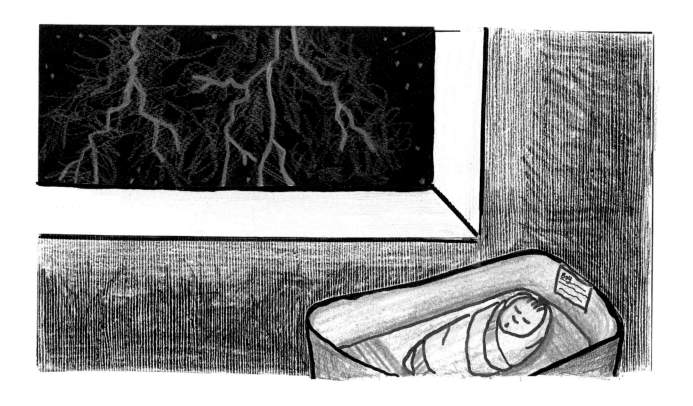

Finn was born on a night filled with lightning and thunder.

Each day brought something new...

Finn soaked it all in as he grew.

His buggy became a window to the world...

Flowers blossomed 'round him and autumn leaves swirled.

The bathtub transformed into an ocean cove...

and fish nibbled on his toes when they dove.

Finn flew up to touch the clouds in his bright blue swing...

chasing the colorful birds to hear them sing.

An enchanting rain shower sprinkled down on his smile...

inviting giggles and belly laughs all the while.

The great outdoors housed an adventure land...

grassy hills and rocky valleys were at his command.

Finn braved the desert winds, shovel in hand...

with sand between his toes and castles so grand.

He galloped across the plains on his horse made of wood...

Finn rode like the wind, as fast as he could!

Finn strolled through the woods and dragged a stick along the way...

He hopped and frolicked in his joyful day of play!

After a smorgasbord of delectable delights...

Finn settled down for a restful night.

Dreams revealed all the adventures he'd had so far...

and more would come, after the evening star!

Made in the USA
Lexington, KY
11 October 2018